Weighing the Elephant

称 大 象

Written by: Jin Honggang
Illustrated by: Wang Guoneng

编文　靳洪刚
绘画　王国能

海豚出版社　北京
DOLPHIN BOOKS　BEIJING

First Edition   1996

ISBN 7-80051-391-2

© Dolphin Books, Beijing, 1996

Published by Dolphin Books
24 Baiwanzhuang Road, Beijing 100037, China

Distributed by China International Book Trading Corporation
35 Chegongzhuang Xilu, Beijing 100044, China
P.O. Box 399, Beijing, China

Printed in the People's Republic of China

Long ago in China during the time of the Three Kingdoms, there was a high official named Cao Cao. He had a son named Cao Chong who was only seven years old.

中国古代三国时期，有一个大官叫曹操。他有个儿子叫曹冲，那年他才刚刚七岁。

One day, someone sent Cao Cao an elephant as a present. Cao Cao wanted very much to know how much the elephant weighed.

一天，有人送给曹操一只大象，他很想知道这只大象有多重。

So he asked his officials: "Who among you can weigh the elephant and find out how much she weighs?" But no one knew how to answer. "Alright then," Cao Cao told them, "you have two days and two days only to find a method."

于是，曹操问官员们："你们谁有办法把大象称称，看它有多重?"可是没有一个人能回答这个问题。"那好吧，限你们两天之内想出办法，把大象称称。"曹操吩咐道。

When they heard this order, the officials were all very worried. "What will we do? Where can we find a scale big enough to weigh an elephant? And if we ever found a scale that big, how could we get the elephant up onto it?" They all heaved a deep sigh feeling helpless at finding the solution.

得到这个命令,官员们都很发愁。"这可怎么办?""我们上哪儿去找这么大的称来称大象呢?""再说,就是有这么大的称,我们又怎么把大象提起来呢?"大家唉声叹气,束手无策。

Cao Chong happened to be playing nearby. When he heard the officials' problem, he went over and said, "Come with me, I know how to do this." The officials looked at the little boy doubtfully: "Are you sure?" And Cao Chong confidently said again, "Come on, follow me!"

正在附近玩耍的曹冲听到后，走过来对官员们说："跟我来，我有办法。"官员们疑惑地看着小曹冲说："真的有办法吗?"曹冲又肯定地说了一次，"你们跟我来好了。"

Leading the elephant, the officials followed Cao Chong to the river. Cao Chong pointed to a boat on the river bank and said, "Put the elephant on the boat."

　　大家牵着大象跟着曹冲来到了河边。曹冲指着河边的船说："把大象牵上船去。"

Everyone pushed and urged the elephant onto the boat, and the boat sank quite a bit deeper into the water under the great weight. Cao Chong asked a man to make a mark on the boat exactly where the water reached.

人们一起把大象推上船，船一下就沉下去一大块。曹冲让人在船帮上画好齐水的记号。

After the boat was marked, Cao Chong told the people to lead the elephant back onto the bank. Then he told them to load stones onto the boat and not stop until the water had again reached the mark.

　　记号画好后，曹冲叫人把大象牵回岸上。然后又叫人往船上放石头，放到水面与船上的记号齐了为止。

Everyone thought this was very, very strange and they said, "What sort of a game is this boy playing?" They didn't understand what Cao Chong was doing, but they did what he said all the same. More and more stones were loaded onto the boat and soon the water was right by the mark.

大家都觉得十分奇怪，说："这个小孩在耍什么鬼把戏呀？"尽管人们没有明白曹冲的用意，但是他们还是照曹冲的要求去做了。石头越装越多，很快水面就跟船上的记号平了。

Cao Chong called out, "That's good, now take the stones back on shore and weigh them one by one. Add up the weight of the stones and you'll have the weight of the elephant."

曹冲喊道:"好了!现在把石头抬下来,一块块称一称,加在一起就是大象的重量了!"

"Oh-ho, now this is a smart young boy!" Everyone there was astonished at Cao Chong's method. And all the officials were very grateful to little Cao Chong for helping them solve their difficult problem.

"啊！好聪明的孩子呀！"在场的人们都被曹冲的办法震惊了。官员们都十分感激小曹冲帮他们解决了一个难题。